Lily

Abigail Thomas

Illustrated by William Low

Henry Holt and Company

New York

Henry Holt and Company, Inc., *Publishers since 1866*, 115 West 18th Street, New York, New York 10011.
Henry Holt is a registered trademark of Henry Holt and Company, Inc. Text copyright © 1994 by Abigail
Thomas. Illustrations copyright © 1994 by William Low. All rights reserved. Published in Canada by
Fitzhenry & Whiteside Ltd., 195 Allstate Parkway, Markham, Ontario L3R 4T8.
ISBN 0-8050-2690-8   First Edition—1994
Printed in the United States of America on acid-free paper. ∞
10 9 8 7 6 5 4 3 2 1

Library of Congress Cataloging-in-Publication Data
Thomas, Abigail.
   Lily / Abigail Thomas; illustrated by William Low.
   Summary: Lily, a dog that likes everything in its place and the same activities
every day, is scared and upset when moving men come and take everything away.
   [1. Dogs—Fiction. 2. Moving, Household—Fiction.]
   I. Low, William, ill. II. Title.
PZ7.T364Li   1994   [E]—dc20   93-14190

For Lizie and Lily, of course
—A. T.

To Allison from Uncle William
—W. L.

Lily is Aunt Eliza's dog. She is black with soft ears and a stubby tail.

She is just the right size for sitting on Eliza's lap with a little left over.

"You're getting big for this," says Eliza, when she is trying to read the newspaper. But she never says, "Get down, Lily." She says, "Good dog, Lily. You are a very good dog."

Lily and Aunt Eliza have always lived in a small apartment in the city of Boston, and everything has always stayed in its rightful spot, just the way Lily likes it.

The soft blue couch. The big yellow chair. The bookcase by the window. And under the piano, where somedays Lily likes to chew her rubber hedgehog.

Lily even has her own special bed, which is a green cushion in a wicker basket. Lily does not like her bed. As soon as Eliza goes to work in the morning, Lily hops up on the yellow chair. She sleeps for a long time.

When she hears Eliza's car door slam, she jumps down and runs to look out the window. Eliza is home!

Lily is happy. She wags her tail. When Lily wags her tail, her whole behind wags too.

"Good dog, Lily," says Eliza. "You are a very good dog."

Every morning and every evening Eliza and Lily go for a
walk on the sidewalk. At the end of the block is a patch of grass.
Lily would like to dig a hole but Eliza says, "No, Lily. Not here."
Still, everything is just how Lily likes it. Everything is where
it belongs.

Then one terrible morning, everything changed.

Even her walk was not the same.

"Come on, Lily," said Eliza. "We're in a hurry today." Lily was busy smelling an interesting stick. Lily did not like to be in a hurry. She sat right down on the sidewalk, and she would not budge. "Come *along,* Lily," said Eliza, and she gave a little tug on the leash.

Poor Lily. She did not like this day. She lay down and put her chin between her paws. She looked up at Eliza with sad eyes.

Eliza picked Lily up in her arms. "We are moving today," she explained. "I have to get us packed." Eliza set Lily down on her special bed. "I need you to be a good dog, Lily," she said. "I need you to stay put."

Lily did not stay put. Instead, she hopped up on the blue couch. "Woof," said Lily. Eliza did not notice. So Lily hopped down from the couch and up on the yellow chair. Scratch, scratch, scratch.

Eliza *still* did not notice. She was not paying any attention to Lily at all! She was too busy. She took the pictures off the wall. She took the books out of the bookcase.

She took the clothes out of the closet and the towels out of the bathroom and the dishes out of the kitchen. She put everything into big boxes. Even Lily's bowl disappeared into a box. Nothing was where it was supposed to be.

Two big men came into the room.
"Hi, pooch," said one of them to Lily.
Nobody had ever called Lily pooch
before and she jumped off the chair
and tried to hide. She watched while
the big men carried everything out
of the room.

The blue couch. The yellow chair.

The bookcase. The table and
the lamp and the boxes.
  As the room got bigger
and bigger, Lily felt
smaller and
smaller.

Finally, the men came back
and took the piano.

Then there was nothing left in the big white room except the little black dog.

"There you are!" said Eliza,
appearing out of nowhere.

She bent down and scooped Lily into her arms. "Time to
go," she said. "Good dog, Lily," said Eliza. "You have been
a very good dog." Lily was too scared to wag her tail.
She shivered instead. Where was everything? What would
happen now?

All the way to
Vermont, Lily shivered
in the car beside Eliza.
Even when she fell
asleep, Lily shivered.

"It's all right, Lily," Eliza said from time to time. "Everything will be all right."

When Lily woke up, Eliza was opening the car door. "Here we are," said Eliza, and Lily hopped out.

At first she was nervous. Everything was so big.

But under her feet was soft grass and more grass and trees as far as she could see. Lily thought there might be interesting things to smell and taste and roll around on. There might be a hole to dig.

"Come along, Lily," said Eliza. "Come inside."

The rooms were big and white. Nothing was
there but Eliza and Lily. But then the truck
pulled up outside and the men began to fill the
house with old familiar things.

The blue couch. The yellow chair. The table.
The lamps. The boxes full of clothes and towels
and dishes. The pictures that went up on
the wall.

The only thing missing was Lily's own bed.
"Oh dear," said Eliza, but Lily
did not mind.

After supper, she was sitting on Eliza's lap where she fit perfectly, with just a little left over.

"You are a good dog," said Eliza, scratching Lily's soft ears. "You are the best dog that ever was." The moon was up, and the stars were out. And everything was in its rightful spot, just the way Lily liked it.